Scary Stories for Halloween Nights

C.B. Colby, John Macklin, Ron Edwards,
Sheryl Scarborough and Sharon McCoy,
Arthur Myers, Margaret Rau

Sterling Publishing Co., Inc.
New York

Library of Congress Cataloging-in-Publication Data Available

2 4 6 8 10 9 7 5 3 1

Published by Sterling Publishing Co., Inc.
387 Park Avenue South, New York, NY 10016

Distributed in Canada by Sterling Publishing
c/o Canadian Manda Group, 165 Dufferin Street
Toronto, Ontario, Canada M6K 3H6
Distributed in Great Britain and Europe by Chris Lloyd at Orca Book Services, Stanley House, Fleets Lane, Poole BH15 3AJ, England
Distributed in Australia by Capricorn Link (Australia) Pty. Ltd.
P.O. Box 704, Windsor, NSW 2756, Australia

Manufactured in the United States of America

Sterling ISBN: 1-4027-2181-1

For information about custom editions, special sales, premium and corporate purchases, please contact Sterling Special Sales Department at 800-805-5489 or specialsales@sterlingpub.com.

CONTENTS

1

Haunted Spaces

Ghost Truck

Just before twelve o'clock on a February night in 1930, a group of men gathered by the side of a lonely lane in northwest England. The men were members of a coroner's jury. They had come out to this desolate spot to seek out a ghost.

Earlier in the month, two men on a motorcycle had crashed in very mysterious circumstances on this same road. The driver died, but his passenger lived to tell the tale. At the inquest, the passenger insisted that they had had to swerve violently because a truck had suddenly backed out of an opening right across their path.

Yet police had inspected the stretch of road—and found there was no opening of any kind in the area from which a truck could have emerged.

"But I saw it as plain as can be!" burst the passenger at the inquest.

"It was probably some form of optical illusion," the coroner commented, but the passenger wouldn't accept the idea.

"There is an opening there. I'll show it to you," he insisted.

"In view of the great number of accidents that have taken place on that particular stretch of road during the past twenty-two months, I think it would be as well if this jury were to examine the scene of the mishap," the coroner declared. "So far, no satisfactory explanation for any of these accidents has been forthcoming, and I think it is time the mystery was solved."

Because every one of the accidents had taken place at night, the coroner added that it might be best if they visited the spot at 'the witching hour.' "If there really is a phantom truck, then it should, according to ghost lore, appear at midnight," he concluded with a smile.

Altogether, three people had been killed and an additional twenty-five injured at the spot in question. Eighteen cars had been involved in crashes, most of the drivers swearing that a vehicle of some sort had suddenly materialized across their path, seemingly from thin air.

Local residents were firmly convinced that a phantom vehicle was to blame. There were ghost ships, phantom armies, and haunted coaches—why not a ghost truck?

"There are ghosts in these parts," they told the reporters. "You can hear them marching up and down the street at night. But when you go to look out of the window, there's nobody there.

"What's more, you can't get a dog to walk along that stretch of road at night. They can see something that sets them howling in terror."

The owner of a pub in the neighborhood went further and declared that every time the ghost walked, an accident took place. "There's no mistaking the tread," he told newspapermen. "It sounds like a very big man clumping along. I've heard it in the courtyard quite often—always late at night and at the full moon. And then, without fail, somebody is found the next morning either dead or dying on the road."

And so, at midnight, February 18, 1930, the motorcycle passenger led the jury to the scene of the accident. Try though he might, however, he could not discover an opening of any sort.

"I can't understand it," he muttered, completely bewildered. "We both saw it backing out of this lane, whatever it was."

"It was probably a patch of mist," remarked one of the jury members.

"This hedge and the wall adjoining caught in the sudden glare of a headlight could very well be mistaken for the back of a truck," ventured another.

The ghost truck did not put in an appearance that night, but soon afterward a huge trailer truck went off the road at the exact same spot.

A few nights after that, a motorcyclist thought he saw something blocking the road ahead. He braked sharply and went careening into the hedge.

And so it went. A member of the Society for Psychical Research spent an entire night by the side of the road, but the phantom eluded him.

Police were convinced that the wall and the hedge were to

blame and had them removed in due course. The accidents became less frequent, but they do still occasionally happen. And it still takes a brave—or unimaginative—person to walk down that lonely lane at midnight when the moon is high...

Madness in the Museum

The Gothic-style building that houses the Fremantle Museum in Western Australia was built in 1863 by convicts as an asylum for the mentally ill. During its heyday it was crowded with these sufferers, among them some who were criminally insane. In 1963, when the vacated buildings were turned into a museum and art center, the rooms were enlarged and modernized and used to display historical relics.

Despite the renovations, the ghosts of those who once lived and died here still seem to haunt the halls. Papers, mops and dusters are sometimes snatched from the hands of employees and tossed around the floor. Knocking is heard in the walls. Footsteps echo up and down the halls.

But the most terrifying things happen in the Discovery Gallery on the second floor. Its story is a dark one. It once contained a block of eight small cells in which violent patients were housed. One of the cells has been preserved to show how badly the criminally insane were treated in the past. The small, cramped cell is equipped with a heavy wooden door that was bolted from the outside.

One day in the late 1970s, a school teacher was taking a group of students through the museum. As she entered the Discovery Gallery, she suddenly began to shove, push and struggle as though she were being attacked by an unseen assailant. All the while she was unable to speak or to hear the questions of her terrified students. At last a museum official was able to lead the teacher out of the room.

The story of the teacher's experience came to the ears of a brash young man who had just been hired by the museum and was visiting it for the first time. We'll call him Alan. He decided he would prove that there were no such things as ghosts by going to the Discovery Gallery and even entering the model cell. But he had no sooner entered the Gallery than he began gasping for breath. He raced down the stairs and out of the building, where he became violently ill.

Alan stayed away from the museum for two months claiming illness. When he returned, he was just as determined as ever to prove the gallery had no ghosts. This time he was able to go only a short way up the stairs when he began gagging again. Scarcely able to catch his breath, he fled the building. Ghosts or no ghosts, Alan had finally had enough. He quit the job and never went back.

But the most terrifying example of the ghostly power in the Discovery Gallery took place the afternoon three schoolgirls drifted into it. When they came to the model cell, two of the girls pushed the third girl inside as a practical joke. They slammed the door shut on her and bolted it.

What followed, according to officials and visitors who were there, was an explosion of supernatural fury. With a roar, something like a great whirlwind came sweeping through, rattling doors and windows, snatching papers from tables and desks and sending them careening around the room. Through all this weird commotion came the ghastly screams of the hysterical girl in the cell.

Finally someone made it to the wooden door, slid back the bolt and led the girl out. At that moment the whirlwind died down. Doors and windows stopped rattling. Papers settled on the floor. Calm returned, but not to the girl. Sobbing and shaking uncontrollably, she tried to tell what had happened to her. But her voice came out a jumble of unintelligible words. Her eyes, glassy with horror, revealed something of what she had experienced, cooped up in that tiny cell with the raging ghost of a long-dead madman.

Room of Sighs

It seemed such a peaceful, comfortable old place, the house in County Down, in Northern Ireland—and so it was. Except in one of the upstairs bedrooms.

My grandfather, Cecil Macklin, rented the house in July of 1912. A few days after moving in, he was shaving at the mirror in his bedroom when he heard it for the first time. From somewhere within that room, a few feet behind him, he heard a loud, shuddering sigh. Yet, when he glanced around, there was nobody there.

At first, he thought he had imagined the whole business. Then he heard it again. But he chose to ignore it. He had an idea that his children were playing a joke on him.

So when he left his room, he crept silently along the passage to his children's bedroom and whipped the door open. To his amazement, the children were all fast asleep.

Of course, he didn't mention the incident to anyone, since he still wasn't sure he had heard anything. But within the next few days he heard the sighing again. It always happened during the evening. Soon, he noticed that the servants in the house came up with all sorts of excuses rather than enter the room, but when he questioned them, all they could tell him was that something there frightened them.

After that, he decided to investigate the phenomenon for

himself. He went up to the room in the afternoon and sat in the rocking chair reading. As evening crept down from the mountainside, he became aware of a coldness that filled the room.

Determined to wait for the sighing to begin, he stayed in the chair until it was too dark to read. Then he heard it again: it almost terrified him out of his wits. For the moaning and sighing seemed to boom out right in his ear, and he realized that it was coming from the chair in which he was sitting!

Springing up, he stared at the chair that was now rocking wildly. Then, all at once, something even weirder happened. The chair stopped rocking—almost as if some invisible hand had halted it!

The heavy sighing was still behind him, and as he moved across the room to light the lamp, it followed him. Suddenly, all his courage deserted him and he rushed for the door—the moaning and breathing pursuing him all the way, until he had wrenched the door open and slammed it behind him.

But as he leaned against it and turned the key in the lock, he could quite clearly hear something snuffling and grunting on the other side of the door.

For the rest of the summer the room was kept locked and none of the family ever went in there again.

But the haunting didn't stop at that.

Some weeks later, when weekend guests were staying at the house, two of the men walking outside saw a strange, pinkish glow coming from the window of that room.

They dashed into the house, shouting "Fire!" and rushed up the stairs. The room was locked, but a strange smell was coming through and they could see a bright light beneath the door.

It was a stout, heavy door, and they couldn't smash it down, so one of the men hurried down the stairs to get an axe. Just as he returned to the top of the stairs, the door flew open. The other man cowered back in horror as a pink light blazed forward. Then a shadow blotted it out and two strong, muscular arms came from the room, pulled him inside, and slammed the door shut.

There was a scream, and the second man began crashing the axe down on the door panels. My grandfather joined him and they forced the door open. They found the room in darkness—and their friend lying unconscious on the floor. They carried him out—and behind them, something sighed—a heavy, despairing sigh, that neither wanted to investigate further!

When their friend came to, he couldn't say what had happened to him. All that he remembered was the door springing open and a dazzling bright light blinding him for a few moments before somebody pulled him into a dark room. Then he fainted.

In the morning, everybody left that house—forever, as it turned out—and spent the rest of the weekend in a nearby inn.

None of the local people were surprised by their vacating the house. What was surprising was that it had only been a few months earlier that the house had first achieved the reputation of being haunted. Before then, it had been occupied by the same family for over 200 years, and during that time it had been a happy home.

Then, early in 1912, after it had been sold, it was being renovated. One of the workmen was alone in that bedroom, plastering part of the wall. Suddenly he heard a sigh. At first, he thought it had been caused by a draft, or the wind outside. Then he realized that it was coming from within that very room—from a few yards away—but there was nobody there. Nothing, except the shadows dancing in the flickering light from his lamp.

But what made the flame flicker? There was nothing to explain it.

Then the rocking chair, which had been absolutely motionless until that moment, started to sway gently back and forth, exactly as if somebody were sitting in it.

From then on, the workmen refused to go into the room except by twos, and then only in daylight.

The house is still there, and it's still occupied, but the people living there don't use the room except to store their unwanted bits and pieces. And the door is still kept locked.

The Dark Evil That Haunts Walsingham House

It was difficult to say just when the Walsingham family realized that there was something different about the house—something evil. Certainly, it was before they went in and opened the shuttered windows.

They hadn't been away that long. It was only 10 days since Howard Walsingham had left the house with his wife, their teenage son and daughters, and cat and dog—to visit with relatives and attend a wedding in Charleston, South Carolina, over 100 miles away.

Their farmhouse, which lay on the outskirts of the small town of Oakville, had always been a happy one. But on this spring day in 1889, everyone felt that something was wrong.

The dog, Don Caesar, refused to enter the place. When young Howard dragged him in, he broke into furious snarling and barking. His back bristled with rage. This happened several times. As the day went on, he continued to act strangely, as if terrified.

Later, after a neighbor and his wife came to welcome them home, Walsingham heard whines and growls from one of the rooms. When he went to investigate, he saw that Don Caesar seemed to have gone mad. The big hound leaped into the air as if going for a man's throat, but suddenly he fell back, as if he had received a heavy blow, and lay motionless on the floor.

When Walsingham picked up the dog, its neck had been broken. It was dead.

That evening, around dusk, the house was suddenly filled with shouts and hideous laughter. This was heard by everybody, including the neighbors, and it put them all in a state of near-panic.

Then Amelia, the older daughter, brushing her hair in front of a mirror, plainly saw a man's hand resting on her shoulder. But there was no reflection of it in the mirror, nor any sign of an arm or body.

Walsingham, in the garden, saw footprints forming on the dust of the path in front of him as he walked. Yet nothing mortal could be seen.

As uncanny and terrifying as these events were, they paled into insignificance before the incident that took place later that evening.

The family and neighbors were sitting at supper when loud, terrible groans started coming from the room above. The sounds stopped, and talk began again, until someone remarked on a stain of what looked like blood on the white tablecloth. Young Howard then pointed to the ceiling. A liquid was slowly dripping down onto the table from a patch of red. It was so like fresh blood that they couldn't finish the meal. Instead, they watched, horrified, as the liquid continued to drip. It occurred to them all that some terrible deed, some ghastly murder, was taking place upstairs.

Walsingham raced upstairs, followed by his son, and flung open the door, dreading what he might see. But the room was empty.

Pulling up the carpet, they found the floorboards soaked with the same red, gruesome liquid that was dripping into the room below. But there was no explanation.

After an uncomfortable night, Walsingham rode into Oakville and gave a sample of the liquid to the local doctor, who examined it under a microscope. It was unquestionably, he said, human blood.

These incidents were too much for the Walsinghams, who soon moved to another side of town.

Questioned about anything unusual that might have taken place before the macabre events, Walsingham did remember one incident. The day before the family left for the wedding, a farmhand asked Walsingham to look at a pile of old dried bones that had been turned up by the plow. Not able to decide whether or not they were human, Walsingham ordered them thrown into a limekiln.

A spiritualist group suggested that the spirit of the man whose bones were treated to such an indignity might have summoned dark forces to his aid to make the place uninhabitable by mortals. It seems unlikely that a pile of dried bones could produce such terrifying phenomena. But, as yet, no one has come up with a better explanation.

The Ghosts of Creek Road

Dark, lonely roads seem to attract ghosts. People claim to have seen a number of them along Creek Road, which winds through the wilderness outside the town of Ojai in Southern California. The road is spooky even in daylight, with the interlocking branches of gnarled live oaks overshadowing it. At night it can be even more eerie. That's when the ghosts come out.

The best known among them is the Charman. Nobody knows his real name. He's called Charman because his body is practically burned to a crisp. Those who have seen him say he's a horrible sight, with flesh peeling away from his bones. His blackened face is a grinning skull from which a few shreds of skin still hang. Some people claim that when he appears he brings with him the sweet stench of burning flesh.

The Charman's anger and pain seem to have accompanied him into death. He has a habit of lunging out of the darkness and attacking anyone walking alone down the quiet road. In 1950 a teenager went for a walk on Creek Road to prove his bravery and came rushing away white-faced, claiming that the Charman had torn his jacket from his back. His story made the papers.

There have been many theories about who the Charman really was. At first people thought he was a fireman who had burned to death in the 1948 fires that raged through the forests surrounding Ojai. Because his body was never found and given a decent burial, he was doomed to walk the shadowy road for all time, taking out his anger on innocent passersby.

This story was disproved when a look at old records showed that no firefighter had been lost in the fire of 1948. Then people said if not a forest fire, an automobile accident must have been the cause of the Charman's fiery death. A few have a much darker theory. They say the Charman could have been the victim of a murderer who torched him and left him to die in the forest. Now filled with rage, he stalks the dark road seeking revenge upon the man who killed him.

The Charman doesn't travel alone on dark, winding Creek Road. A young horsewoman has been seen there on the anniversary of her death. She rides recklessly down Creek Road until she reaches a place called the Curve, which is treacherously sharp. Here the horse stumbles, rears and throws her. She falls, breaks her neck and dies instantly. Then, in the next few minutes, she is back again, riding at breakneck speed to the killer curve. People say that she repeats this ride until day breaks and she can rest for another year.

A third ghost is a young bride who chooses the anniversary of her death to hitchhike down the old road in a white wedding dress stained with blood. No one knows who she was or why she was killed on her wedding day, or why she chooses to hitchhike on this spooky road to commemorate the murder.

The fourth ghost in this strange assortment is a motorcyclist. He rides pell-mell down the treacherous road over and over again. It's hard to understand how he negotiates it so skillfully, because, you see, he has no head.

The Phantom Biplane

On May 27, 1963, Sir Peter Masefield, well known in aviation lore, was flying a DeHavilland Chipmunk from Dalcross to Shoreham, England. Masefield was going by way of the abandoned Royal Air Force airfield at Montrose. As he approached the airfield, he suddenly saw before him an ancient biplane, a plane with two pairs of supporting wings placed one above the

other. It was the type of plane the RAF used for training before World War I.

The plane was close enough so that Masefield could see the aviator, who was dressed in a leather helmet, goggles and the silken scarf that was part of every old-time aviator's wardrobe. As Masefield stared, the biplane's upper right wing broke loose from its struts. The craft spun crazily in midair and then spiraled to the ground and crashed.

In horror, Masefield landed at a nearby golf course among a group of startled players. He shouted to them for help. Though the golfers had heard and seen nothing of a crash, they followed Sir Peter to the abandoned airfield. It was empty.

The experience was so disturbing to Masefield that he made inquiries at the Accidents Investigation Committee headquarters of the RAF. He found two entries dated June 2 and June 10, 1913. They described an accident that had taken place on the 27th of May, 1913. A training plane flown by Lieutenant Desmond Arthur had lost its upper right wing and crashed at Montrose field on that date.

Young Lieutenant Arthur was Irish, from County Clare. When he died, he was given a burial with full military honors. But in 1916 an official report attributed the loss of his plane to negligence and his memory was blackened.

From that time on, the ghost of Lieutenant Arthur was seen at No. 2 Mess Hall, where he had lived. It was always dressed in the full uniform of an aviator. It appeared so often that it became known as the "Irish Apparition."

Soon the ghost began to show up in other parts of the base. When guards challenged the ghost, it would disappear before their eyes, sending them fleeing in terror.

The story of the ghost spread through the RAF and beyond. It began appearing in newspapers across England, where it came to the attention of an editor for a British flying magazine. He concluded that the dead aviator wanted his name cleared and insisted that the RAF make a further investigation into the cause of the crash. This time the RAF found that the blame lay not on the aviator but on the poor maintenance of the aircraft. The honor of the dead aviator restored, the Irish Apparition made its last appearance on earth in January of 1917.

But the daredevil young pilot must have still been haunting the airwaves above Montrose, when on May 27, 1963—the fiftieth anniversary of his death—he repeated his spectacular crash for the benefit of Sir Peter Masefield, one of Great Britain's most renowned aviators.

2

Ghostly Animals

The Black Horse of Sutton

There are stories of phantom horses from all around the world. Usually, these horses are white or black. Sometimes they are never seen—only the clatter of their hooves is heard, along with the rattle of spurs and the smart crack-crack of the whip in the ghostly rider's hands. The horses gallop through history carrying important messages to kings and generals or their ladies.

The Black Horse of Sutton is unique in that it appeared only to a humble woman, old Mrs. Sutton. She and her husband had established a homestead in the bush land outside the town of Goulburn in New South Wales, Australia. It was an isolated place removed many miles from the nearest human settlement. In that general area it was known as the Sutton Homestead, or just plain Sutton.

One spring day, Mr. Sutton had to ride into Goulburn to negotiate a land deal. He left Mrs. Sutton behind on the lonely homestead, promising to return as soon as possible. Those were the days when there were few roads. Transportation depended on the horse. Even the mail might take a month or more to arrive. Mrs. Sutton knew she might have a long wait before her.

Day by day, she waited eagerly for her husband's return. She had no way of knowing when he would be back, except by the sound of the hoof beats of his returning horse. So one evening, a week after he left, when she heard the distant rat-a-tat-tat of galloping hooves, her heart leapt with happiness. She was sure that her husband was at last on his way home.

The hoof beats came closer and closer. They stopped at the outer gate. She heard the horse turning as if the rider were closing the gate behind him and the click of the gate as it closed.

Now the thundering hoof beats were galloping down the drive and around the corner of the house. Suddenly, a magnificent black stallion came into view. But, to Mrs. Sutton's horror, it was riderless. On hooves that hammered out a staccato beat, the horse galloped directly toward the shuddering woman. She

cried out, terrified. But at the last minute the great beast shied away from her and trampled into the house, where it disappeared. The hoof beats echoed in the ranges of distant mountains. Fainter and fainter they sounded until finally they disappeared altogether.

The next day a messenger arrived to tell Mrs. Sutton that on his way home the evening before, her husband had been thrown by his plodding farm horse. He had been found lying dead by the side of the road while the horse grazed quietly nearby.

Had the black stallion not been riderless after all? Was the soul of Mr. Sutton astride the horse—invisible but still present—as he rode home for the last time?

Twice more the specter horse appeared to Mrs. Sutton. Once it came to announce the death of her elder son, killed in the Boer War in South Africa. Later, it came to tell her of her younger son's accidental death.

When old Mrs. Sutton died, the homestead she and her husband loved so much was demolished. Progress transformed it into a hamlet of small homes. Fine roads and automobiles linked the inhabitants to the outside world.

And the Black Horse of Sutton gallops no more.

The Expanding Dog

Several years ago, when I visited the Chumash Indian reservation in the Santa Ynez valley, I met an elderly woman known to her friends as Aunt Minnie. She told me about a very strange experience she had had one night when walking home from a visit with a friend.

It was a pleasant summer evening with a young moon riding low in the east. Suddenly, Aunt Minnie heard a whispering sound behind her. At first she thought it was a breeze rustling the leaves of the live oaks. But when she looked up, she saw nothing stirring. She turned around to find out if something was following her. She saw a tiny puppy trotting along behind her.

It didn't look dangerous, but there was something very strange about it. It was no larger than a small matchbox! Whoever heard of a dog that small?

Aunt Minnie quickened her steps, just wanting to get home. But the whispering sound continued to pursue her, and it kept growing louder. She looked back again.

The puppy had grown. It was much larger now, the size of a big cat. A real dog couldn't grow that fast, she thought. Aunt Minnie began to run, but always behind her came the whispering, whispering. She kept glancing over her shoulder—and every time she looked, the dog was bigger, and it was close on her heels.

By the time she reached the gate of her home, the dog was almost as large as a pony and had turned jet black. Huge red eyes glared at her. Fangs gleamed white in slavering, open jaws. Aunt Minnie's knees were so wobbly she could hardly walk. Somehow she managed to push through the gate, stagger to her front door, open it and collapse inside.

Her husband, Ben, helped her to a chair. She sat, pale and

shivering, unable to say a word. Ben got a blanket and wrapped her up in it, but she still went on shaking and her teeth were chattering. At last she managed to tell Ben about the dog.

Ben grabbed his gun and ran out to shoot the creature, but it had disappeared. He could hear its faint baying in the hushed night—a ghostly baying that he realized could only come from a ghost dog.

"That's what it was," he told me, "a ghost dog with a ghost shaman for its master. It's been seen by others around here since. We know where it comes from—that old graveyard where the shamans did their black magic.

"No use to shoot at it. I just put my gun away. And told my Minnie she was plenty lucky to get away so quick inside."

The Sacred Cat

His fatal encounter with the mummy case was not the first terrifying situation that archaeologist Gordon Richardson had faced with an object from one of the Egyptian tombs. There had been his spine-chilling experience with the sacred cat.

The mummy of the cat was contained in a small coffin when native workmen brought it out of the tomb of one of the Pharaohs. Why they then put the unopened mummy case in Richardson's hotel room remains a mystery. They didn't tell him about it. And when he returned to his room after dark, he stumbled over the small coffin and nearly broke his neck.

The coffin was made in the shape of a sitting cat and was in two shell-like sections. Inside would be a mummified cat sitting upright, embalmed and wrapped in cloth.

Richardson left the case where it was. When he went to bed it was still sitting there in the center of the room, staring at him with its painted eyes.

In the middle of the night, he was awakened by a noise like a pistol shot. As he sprang up, a large gray cat sprang across his bed, clawed his hand viciously, and dashed away through the open window.

By the time Richardson recovered from his shock, he was startled to see by the light of the moon that the two sides of the coffin had burst apart and were still rocking to a standstill on the floor. Between them sat the sacred embalmed cat, swathed in bandages.

When he scrambled out of bed, a chill swept over him. The bandages on the mummified cat had been savagely torn open at the throat—as if by an animal clawing its way to freedom.

Richardson knew that ancient Egyptians believed that the souls of the dead left the body by way of the throat. But another idea was forming in his mind—one that belied a lifetime of rational thinking and all his scientific training. He could not help toying with the seemingly preposterous idea that the sacred

cat had torn itself free from its bonds—and that the gray cat that attacked him was the mummified cat's escaping spirit.

Of course, Richardson said later, there was a perfectly straightforward explanation for the entire experience. It was possible that the brittle wooden coffin had broken open because of the accidental kick he had given it—and perhaps because of the change of atmosphere from the dry desert to the more humid banks of the Nile.

And the gray cat probably had wandered into his bedroom from the village, possibly through the open window.

And the injury to the embalmed cat's throat? That might have happened when the ancient undertaker, just before sealing up the cat's coffin, stole the jewel that he knew would be there under the wrappings.

Possible? What do you think?

Dreamtime Visitor

An Aboriginal family living in a small town in South Australia went on a camping trip in the Coorong, a coastal strip of swamp and dunes about 87 miles long. Low tide along the Coorong exposes wide expanses of salt flats. That night the Aboriginal family was out spotlighting on the flats. To spotlight, they shone their powerful hand-held flashlights across the flats to pick up crabs and other sea creatures.

All at once, the powerful lights illuminated a trail of giant footprints crossing the muck. They were spaced about four feet apart. The Aborigines looked out over the flats to see what had made the tracks, and found themselves staring into two shining eyes the size of automobile headlights, and they were spaced almost the same distance apart. But their eerie sheen was unlike any car lights the Aborigines had ever seen. As they looked into the huge eyes, the terrified family felt a strange tingling sensation traveling through their bodies, like an electric charge. They turned and fled.

At first the neighbors of the family scoffed at the story, calling it a wild fairy tale. Then some of those neighbors went camping on the Coorong and saw for themselves the great eyes staring at them and felt the same electric chill of fear. Other reports began to filter in.

One came from Cooberpedy, some 700 miles to the north of the Coorong. Cooberpedy is a little opal-mining town in Australia's inland desert region where rainfall averages less than three inches a year. Only the hardiest desert growths can exist there. Most large creatures would find it difficult to survive.

There aren't many homes above ground in Cooberpedy. People use bulldozers to dig cave homes in the low hills that surround the town. These homes are beautifully furnished and quite comfortable. Josh and his family live in one of them. Sometimes he and his neighbors get together for an evening of bridge.

One night the bridge players were gathered in Josh's home, a game in progress. Suddenly Josh felt a tingling like a strong electric charge run through his body. The hair on his arms stood up. His scalp crawled. He jumped to his feet and ran to the front door. Flinging it open, he stepped outside.

The sky above him was velvet black, sparkling with desert stars against which the humps of hills rose in scallops. Then he turned to see two great luminous eyes staring down upon him from the summit of the hill at whose base he stood. The eyes were set about four feet apart and there was a strange glitter in them. Josh had seen that glow before. It was the same glitter that appeared in the eyes of his cat when it was stalking a mouse.

Shaking with terror, Josh slammed the door shut and told his neighbors what he had seen. But, by the time they rushed out to get a look at the eyes, the creature had disappeared.

What animal has such huge, piercing eyes? None in this world that we know of, that's certain. But the Aborigines have an answer.

"They're our animal ancestors, the dreamtime heroes," they explain. "We use secret rituals to enter the dreamtime in which they still live. So why can't they leave the dreamtime to visit us? And when they do, better watch out. Some of those fellas can be pretty fierce and mean, if you make them mad."

3

SPIRITED SPIRITS

A Very Firm Disbeliever

A wealthy young couple had built a large, elaborate house near Gulfport, Mississippi. Their teenage daughter committed suicide there. The parents were, of course, extremely sorrowful. But only a few days later, they fled the house taking a minimum of clothing, never to return.

Their hasty departure did not suggest sorrow as much as it did extreme fear. Rumors quickly spread that the house was now haunted.

Fran Franklin, now a professor of journalism at the University of Arkansas, was nine years old at the time. She had a favorite aunt, Harriet Gibbons, who was an unusual person. Tiny—only four feet tall—she was the editor of a daily newspaper in Mississippi, and she had very definite opinions. She knew the young couple, and ridiculed their flight as pure superstition.

"There is no such thing as a ghost," Harriet often said.

She said she planned to stay in the house overnight to prove there was nothing to be frightened of. Fran asked if she could go along, and her aunt agreed.

So one night, the two let themselves into the house with a key that Harriet had gotten from friends. They set two chairs in the front hallway and sat down to wait for something to happen. Around midnight, something happened.

Upstairs, they heard a door close. Then they heard what sounded like footsteps coming down the hall. Fran looked at the top of the wide staircase, expecting to see a ghostly figure, but she saw nothing. However, she could hear the footsteps coming down the stairs! As they reached the bottom of the stairs, Fran could see a depression in the carpet. When the footsteps reached the marble floor, they clicked across the foyer. They clicked down the hall to a set of double doors that opened into a music room. The doors opened.

Fran was terrified. She looked at her little aunt for a clue. Harriet sat unmoving, her face expressionless.

The footsteps continued across the floor of the music room, stopping at a piano that was visible from the foyer. As Fran and Harriet watched, the piano stool came back. The top covering the piano keys was raised, revealing the keyboard. A short concert of three pieces by Chopin came from the piano.

Then the music stopped. The cover of the keyboard came back down. The piano stool moved back to its original position.

The sound of steps came out of the room. The double doors closed. The steps tapped back across the marble foyer to the foot of the stairs. There they hesitated, as though the unseen performer was momentarily observing her audience of two. Then the footsteps went back up the stairs, and back down the upstairs hall. Fran and her aunt heard a door upstairs close.

Aunt Harriet turned to Fran. "It's time to go now," she said.

As they were driving back to their motel, Fran got up the courage to ask Aunt Harriet what she thought of all this.

"There is no such thing as a ghost," Aunt Harriet replied.

A Very Strange Telephone Call

Mammoth Cave National Park, in Kentucky, contains perhaps the most famous collection of caves in the world. According to many people who work there as guides, or who are among the

2,000,000 tourists who visit the caves each year, there are ghosts in those caverns.

The most convincing witnesses might well be members of the Cave Research Foundation, which numbers some 650 scientists who investigate caves all over the United States. Their headquarters are at Mammoth Park. Most CRF members are professors at universities, not the sort of people who would make up stories about ghostly experiences. But things happen. As one CRF member put it:

"We're a bunch of hard-nosed people. Most of us who have had these experiences are not believers in ghosts, ordinarily. We just describe the facts and let others decide."

Two CRF members who had a chilling experience are Dr. Will White, a professor of geochemistry at Pennsylvania State University, and Dr. George Deike, a government scientist. They were investigating Crystal Cave, which is no longer open to the public. However, it had once been open to tourists, and there was an old army field telephone down in the cave.

"I guess they used it," White says, "to let the guides know some people were coming, to tell them to wake up."

On this day, White and Deike, on their way through the cave to do some geological exploration, were walking by this broken-down phone—when suddenly, it rang! The two scientists were too startled, perhaps too fearful, to stop. They kept walking down the passageway.

White says, "When we got about 200 feet farther on, the

phone rang again! We looked at each other for a moment, and then we ran back. I picked up the old phone and answered. It was one of those old-fashioned army phones with a sort of butterfly switch on it.

"What I heard sounded like a phone sounds when it's off the hook and there are people in the room. You hear the sounds of voices, but you can't tell what they are saying. I said hello or something like that. And on the other end there's a startled gasp. And that was all. No one responded. The line was dead."

Astonished, the two scientists noticed that the phone was attached to a rusty, twisted phone line. They traced it back to the mouth of the cave, and out to a weathered shack that had once been a ticket office. But the phone line ended there. It was attached to nothing!

Had Dr. White heard the sounds of another world?

Partying with the Ouija Board

It was a frosty February night in 1963, and many of the guests had come to the party in Norfolk, England, from towns as far as 50 or 60 miles away. Four had come a mere 30 miles. These four discovered at 11:30 that night that they had been selected to die.

It was a Ouija that gave the message. All that is needed for a Ouija is a board that shows the letters of the alphabet in a semi-circle, as well as the words "Yes" and "No," and a light wineglass. To work it, the operator positions the glass upside down in the center and touches the base with one finger. Presumably, the spirits of the dead channel enough energy into the glass to move it across the table to spell out messages or answer Yes or No.

The Ouija board had become the fad of the moment. The usual light-hearted questions were asked and the glass rumbled around, giving obedient answers.

Mike Chambers, who had just joined the group, was worried about driving home. Addressing the air above the table, he asked, "What sort of road conditions will there be?"

After a pause, the glass gave a surprisingly clear answer:

Ice patches . . . bend.

This direct message inspired more questions: "How far away?"

Many miles.

"Will there be an accident?" Yes.

"Will anyone be killed?"

Four people . . . people four.

Then the glass appeared to lose interest and meandered around the board. But the group was fired with a morbid interest.

"What is the nearest landmark to the accident?"

Marsham Arms.

The Marsham Arms was an inn midway between Norwich and the little fishing town of Sheringham where the party was being held. Furthermore, it stood on a bend near a crossroads, fulfilling other factors the Ouija had noted.

Two more questions were asked that would set the seal of doom. The first was "What time is this accident to take place?"

After much wandering and slithering, the glass spelled out One o'clock.

Mike Chambers had already decided to get home by 1:30, which meant he had to leave the party by 12:15. He realized that, if he followed this schedule, he would be rounding the bend on which the fateful Marsham Arms stood at just about one o'clock.

Hardly knowing that he was asking the clinching question, he dumbly watched the glass move to yes. His question: "Will anyone in this room be involved?"

Since Mike's car was the only one going in the direction of Norwich, it was obvious to everyone in the room that he and his friends were the ones referred to by the wineglass.

The party had died. As the guests filed out the door, one of them turned and said to the hostess: "Why not keep Mike and the others back a little longer? That way they won't be near the Marsham Arms when the accident is supposed to happen."

It seemed such a good idea that Mike was glad to agree. He started out exactly an hour after he had intended to leave.

During the homeward journey, the prophecy was apparently forgotten. But not for long. Rounding a bend a few miles from Sheringham, Mike's small car skidded wildly. In a shaky voice, one of the girls said, "Phew, ice patches, just like it said."

Heedful of the ice menace, Mike drove more slowly. At last they came to the rise that overlooked the Marsham Arms Inn.

The car radio was playing a pop tune. The road, as they gazed down at the sleeping inn, descended at a shallow angle until, curving left, it ran onto the crossroads. The ice on it glittered in the moonlight.

There had been no accident that night. There were no skid marks, no wrecked cars.

As they entered the wide bend, the music from the radio stopped. An announcer's voice came over the air.

"This is the American Forces Network, Frankfurt," the voice said. "The time is now exactly one o'clock Central European time."

As he spoke, Chambers and his friends saw the headlights of another car flashing past the stark trees that lined the road. The car was moving too fast to round the bend with the ice they knew to be on it.

Reg, sitting behind the driver, said it "It really is one o'clock! We forgot: the clock goes back for winter!"

At that time the British still kept up their wartime practice of moving the time backwards or forward an hour in winter and summer. The four realized that one o'clock in Germany was in reality one o'clock in England, not an hour later as their clocks said.

The oncoming car, a Jaguar, roared over the crossroads directly in their path. Someone shouted, "Brake—for God's sake!"

Mike knew better. "I can't!" he cried. Braking on that treacherous surface would throw the car into an uncontrollable skid. There was only one way to slow down, and it was only slightly less dangerous. Mike double declutched and changed gear from fourth to second. The engine howled, the gears screamed, and the car shuddered as its forward motion was slowed by its own engine going slower than the wheels it drove.

At that moment, the other car hit the ice. Its front slipped around, headlights glaring. The massive hood of the Jaguar swung around and pointed toward them. Swift as a bullet, it slithered across the road, hit the bank mere feet in front of them and bounced clear. Then it bounced again briefly before plunging its gleaming snout once more into the scarred earth.

At that moment, Mike's car crept forward through the gap between the bank and the Jaguar, as the other car bounced off. Mike cleared it, just as the giant sports car lunged forward and hit into the space where Mike's car had been seconds before. Had it hit their flimsy car, they would have been steamrollered. Surely, they all would have been killed!

Those are the facts. The direful prophecy was fulfilled in most ways: There were ice patches and there was certainly one outside the Marsham Arms. There was an accident and it did involve four of the people at the party. It took place at one o'clock. But no one was killed. The other driver merely suffered a concussion.

How much had reading the future altered it? If he had not known of the future accident, Mike Chambers would have left at the time he originally intended, not an hour later. But having been alerted, he took a risk with his car that he would not normally have taken. He said later that had it not been for the warning, he would have expected the other driver to slow down in time.

Of course, there is another question, and it is real and ominous. Is it certain that the accident was due to happen on the night of the party? Or might it take place on some frosty night in the future . . . ?

The Haunted Museum

One of the favorite public haunted places in Toronto, Canada, is a museum called the Mackenzie House, but the people who work there don't seem to enjoy it as much as casual visitors do. In fact, the people who take care of the place often find it pretty scary.

The house was once the home of William Mackenzie, who was the mayor of Toronto, but he made so many enemies that for a time he had to flee Canada and take refuge in the United States. Now that he is safely dead, he seems to have returned to his Toronto home. Some caretakers have seen him.

One, a Mrs. Edmunds, tells of seeing the apparition of a small, bald man in an old-fashioned frock coat. This certainly

sounds like Mackenzie, although in life he usually wore a red wig. Perhaps he has mislaid it in the next world. Or maybe he has become less vain about his appearance.

Mackenzie published a small newspaper, and the press on

which he printed it is still in the cellar. It is kept locked, but many staff members swear they have heard rumbling below that sounds suspiciously like an old-time printing press going full tilt.

Another ghost, more belligerent toward the living than Mackenzie, is that of a woman. Mrs. Edmunds has had her problems with this one. She tells of awakening at night to see a woman with dark brown hair and a narrow face, leaning over and staring at her intently. A few months later, Mrs. Edmunds awoke again to see the ghostly woman. This time the ghost struck her in the face, giving her a black eye.

The Edmunds children keep seeing the ghost of a woman in the bathroom, a ghost that disappears on being sighted. Plants in the house are often watered mysteriously—and sometimes carelessly, for the curtains are splashed with mud.

It's not on record exactly how long the Edmunds put up with these shenanigans before moving out. However, it is on record that other caretakers have also had their troubles. Many have reported that the toilets flushed by themselves and that water taps turned on when there was no one—alive—around to do this.

A caretaker named Mrs. McCleary says she often feels as though a ghost is putting its arms around her. However, since the spirit remains invisible, it's anyone's guess whether it is Mackenzie or the lady ghost.

Whenever renovation work is done at the house, workmen come up with a whole new batch of anecdotes about the place. Often objects such as sawhorses, ropes, and drop sheets are found in the morning to have been moved around, even though the building had been locked all night. And one workman, Murdo MacDonald, gained fame when he was first into the house one morning and found a hangman's noose over a stairway.

It's no wonder that the Mackenzie House is one of the favorite stops on Halloween ghost tours in Toronto.

4

SKIRMISHES WITH THE SUPERNATURAL

Demon Tree

A lot of people didn't like the tall, powerfully built Dutch civil engineer Jan Bekker, for he was a pretty hard character and he had stepped on a good many toes. But everyone admitted that whatever his faults, Bekker was a determined man who got things done.

It was just before World War II and Bekker was in charge of a construction unit, composed mainly of native labor. He had been hired to build a road along the mountainous west coast of Sumatra between Cota Raja and Sibolga. There had been the usual snags, but work was going ahead according to plan.

One morning, Bekker received two visitors—the headman and witch doctor of the village—both in a state of agitation. Bekker managed to make out that they wanted him to alter the road's course in order to avoid a grove of tamarind trees, the next target for Bekker's bulldozers. The men said that the trees were taboo—and that the tallest one was the home of a demon named Subarjo, who would bring down a terrible vengeance on anyone who disturbed him.

Bekker had heard some of his men murmuring fearfully and now he gave a loud snort of anger. Facing them, he bellowed: "I fear neither man nor demon. And to prove it, I am going to pull down those trees—starting with the biggest one!"

Unlike the headman, whose face was contorted with fear, the witch doctor showed no emotion. He stared impassively at Bekker for a few seconds, then picked up a stick and drew a line on the earth across the road's intended course.

"Your road will not be built beyond this point," he said calmly, then turned and strode away.

Bekker ordered his men to fasten a chain around the biggest tamarind and attach it to one of the heavy tractors. Slowly, the big machine began to take the strain—and at that moment there was a loud, vicious crack. Bekker ducked just in time to avoid

the broken end of the chain. It went whistling past and smashed the skull of one of the laborers.

At the same instant, a scream of agony rang out. The tractor had veered to one side and crushed a second workman under its tracks.

While the men were being buried, the witch doctor and the headman returned. "Two lives have already been lost because of the wrath of Subarjo," the witch doctor said. "Once again I must ask you to leave his spirit in peace and to turn the road aside."

Bekker's patience snapped. "Now, listen," he shouted, "my job is to build this road—and I'm going to do it on time and as planned, even if I have to uproot every blasted tree in Sumatra!"

Bekker's men were terrified by this time, and it took a great deal to persuade them to return to work. But eventually they went back.

Once again, chains were fastened around the tree and the big tamarind creaked and groaned as the tractors took the strain. An electric, fearful atmosphere hung over the spot as the men watched breathlessly. To them—and to Bekker, too—it seemed as though the tree was fighting back, resisting the pull of the tractor with uncanny strength. But at last it gave a loud groan, as though of despair, and came shuddering up out of the earth. And as it did so, the workmen recoiled in sheer horror.

For there, entwined firmly among the roots, was a human skeleton.

Even Bekker was taken aback—but only for a moment. Striding forward, he surveyed the pitiful bones—and then turned to face his men. "There is your demon—no wonder he could not rest in peace. Look—he is pierced through by the roots. Take these bones and bury them somewhere else in a quiet place where he will no longer be in torment. We start work again on the road in the morning."

When he finished speaking, Bekker noticed that his men seemed relieved. Some of them were even smiling. He turned to see what effect his words had on the witch doctor, but the man was gone.

Bekker had an uneasy feeling, though, that his victory had not been as complete as he might have wished.

Even so, he wasn't prepared for the shock that awaited him the following morning. At the exact spot where the witch doctor had drawn his line in the dust, the ground was split by a chasm several yards in length and three feet in width. Other smaller cracks radiated outwards toward the grove of tamarinds. The entire surface of the ground was scarred with them. And they were natural—not man-made—as Bekker suspected at first.

How or why the cracks had appeared, literally overnight, was beyond Bekker. He only knew that he could never build his road straight through the tamarind grove now.

The tamarind grove still stands, and the road that Bekker built curves around it in a wide loop that the local inhabitants call Subarjo's Bend. And a few yards from the trees, the bones of Subarjo himself lie still, peaceful and undisturbed, in the spot where Bekker laid them.

The legend of the demon tree has been forgotten.

Portrait of a Ghost

It was the summer of 1913, and Lebrun, a promising young artist, had only been in Paris for a few weeks. A shy man, especially in the company of women, it took some courage for him to speak to the young girl he saw standing beneath the street lamp in Montmartre. She was looking about her so helplessly—

so obviously uncertain of her whereabouts—that Lebrun finally decided to go to her assistance.

She turned toward him—and his first reaction was astonishment, because he had never seen a more beautiful face! And instead of offering to assist her, he found himself begging her to pose for him.

For several moments she stared at him with a puzzled, frightened expression in her eyes. Then, slowly, she replied:

"A portrait would take several sittings and my time here is very short. Tonight I am with you—but tomorrow I have no idea where—"

Lebrun resolved to finish the painting in one night, and he pleaded so hard that she finally nodded and walked along silently beside him.

When they reached his studio, he set to work at once. She was a perfect study in black and white; her face had a pale, almost deathly hue about it and her clothes were coarse and black. She had a black band high on her throat, and when Lebrun asked her to remove it, she stared at him in terror—and shook her head.

As Lebrun worked through the early hours of that morning, the girl sat perfectly still, perfectly silent.

The first cold light of the new day was over the horizon when Lebrun finished painting. It was a perfect likeness, except for the black band, which he had decided not to incorporate into the picture.

The girl left without even saying goodbye. Lebrun hurried after her, but she had disappeared into the early-morning gloom. And apart from the sound of her footsteps dying away in the distance, it was almost as if she had never existed.

Later that day his landlady came to the studio to collect Lebrun's rent. She took one look at the portrait on the easel and exclaimed, "What a good likeness of Gretel Pederson! You must have seen her photograph in the papers after she was guillotined for murdering her parents and her husband."

Lebrun stared at her. He hadn't heard about the murder and surely had not seen the girl's photograph.

After pacing his room for hours, he decided that he must have been overworking. The whole thing must have been a figment of his imagination—he must have glanced at her photograph in the papers and somehow it had registered in his subconscious.

Just as he was deciding to take things easier, he heard a knocking at his door. It was Julien Sant, an artist friend.

"Lebrun, you can call me a madman if you like—but last night I saw a ghost!"

Sant went on: "It was early evening, about eight o'clock, in the streets near here. There was a young girl and I was obsessed by the thought that I had seen her somewhere before. I just saw her as I passed, but I could never forget that beautiful face.

"Today I went along to the newspaper files, and I saw her photograph. It was Gretel Pederson!"

Lebrun said nothing. Instead he pointed to the picture.

"That's her, all right," said Sant. "But when I saw her she had a high black band around her throat."

Sant added, "And that's not all. I found out that last night was the anniversary of her death . . . !"

The Corpse That Walked Away to Die Again

The fiercest blizzard Scotland had known for over 50 years had been raging for almost four days in February, 1963, when Joe Turnbull's truck ran into a snow drift high on the remote Beattock Summit in Lanarkshire. There were hundreds of other vehicles abandoned along the road.

Turnbull realized that if he stayed where he was, it might be days before he was reported missing, and by then, it would be too late. So he set out to walk to the nearest village.

The whirling snow, hurled at him by a biting cold wind, made it impossible to see more than a few feet in front of him. That was why he didn't see the body lying facedown in the center of the road until he stumbled over it.

Slowly, Turnbull freed the body of a bearded young man from the freezing snow and wrapped his red, brightly patterned scarf around the head to protect it from the cold. The man appeared to be dead.

Turnbull wasn't sure about that, though, and he couldn't walk away and leave the man lying there, because if he weren't dead, he soon would be.

Lifting the unconscious man onto his shoulders, Joe started trudging through three-foot-deep snow drifts to Beattock village. It was almost two miles away, but now two lives depended upon his succeeding.

Some time later, when he was almost fainting from exhaustion, he heard voices and saw the gleam of flashlights. To his relief, two men came striding through the snow. When they saw him almost on his knees with the body across his shoulders, they hurried to assist him.

The darkness, the thickly falling snow, and their hooded jackets hid their faces, but as they took the unconscious—or dead—man from Turnbull, they exchanged details.

They, too, were truck drivers, they said. And when Turnbull

explained about the body, they offered to take it with them to a railway station a few miles across the fields. Turnbull was invited to accompany them, but since he could see the lights of the village, he decided to press on.

Then the two strangers, carrying the limp body between them, disappeared into the storm. And disappeared is the only word to describe what followed. For neither the truck drivers nor the "corpse" were ever seen again.

Joe Turnbull reported the incident to the police, but when they checked with the trucking companies the two strangers were supposed to work for, they found no record of any people with those names ever having been employed. As the storm slackened off, police launched a search for the two men and their burden.

There was always the danger that they had all perished in the blizzard, but no bodies answering their descriptions were discovered. And no men had reached the railway station either that night or in the 48 hours afterward.

Then there was the scarf that Turnbull had wrapped around the "corpse's" head. It had still been there when the other men carried him off, but during the intensive police hunt all over the moors, the scarf was never recovered.

But it was seen again! A motorist who had abandoned his vehicle a few hours later that night, several miles on the other side of Beattock village, later told police how he and his wife had met a young man answering that description. He had been bearded and was wearing a brightly patterned red scarf around his head!

The three of them had walked together toward the village, but somehow during the height of the blizzard, the young man had fallen behind. And although they called out to him and hunted back along the road for a few hundred yards, they failed to find him again.

Soon afterward people started reporting a ghost on Beattock Summit—the ghost of a young, bearded man wearing a colorful scarf around his head. The man stands at the roadside trying to thumb a lift from passing cars. Whenever a car pulls up, the young man vanishes.

Death Watch

From the time John Phillips entered the hospital in September, 1952, until his death a few months later, the hospital staff at St. Olive's, in the town of Biddeford in Devon, England, became increasingly alarmed by strange events surrounding the patient. Phillips was an old man in his late 70s, terribly confused and incapable of carrying on a sensible conversation.

Often, under the ward's dim, orange night lights, the atmosphere would appear to be alive and full of movement around John's bed—like heat waves, wavering and fluctuating. But it was the soft persistent voices that sent the night nurses rushing out of the ward in terror. Each time anyone investigated to find out who was talking to Phillips, the old man was always fast asleep. And when any of the staff crept up to the bed to listen to the voices, which were always indistinguishable, the noise would stop abruptly.

A student nurse received a severe reprimand from the night nurse when she reported that she had heard a large animal padding around the ward, but when the older nurse approached the ward, she too heard the clicking of claws on the hard, polished floor. When she called for help, two doctors and a night porter rushed into the ward to catch the animal, but a thorough search revealed nothing.

Over the next few weeks, nurses often turned up the main lights, crawled about on all fours, and peered under the rows

of beds in an attempt to track down the animal. Often the swift, stealthy padding appeared to brush past them. And then they would hear heavy breathing and smell a strong animal odor.

Patients frequently heard the creature also, and many asked that Phillips be removed to a private room. But because of a shortage of beds, this was not possible. The hospital board finally dismissed the footsteps as being either rats running under the flooring, creaking timbers—or just plain imagination.

On a Wednesday morning, 12 days after Phillips had been put in the ward, there came a manifestation that could not be rejected so easily.

Two young nurses were startled to see a head peeping out from behind the heavy, lined curtains drawn across the window at the head of Phillips' bed. The features were those of a young man with dark, curly hair, and they had never seen him before!

Since visitors were not allowed in the wards at six in the morning, the nurses hurried to the window, and as they did, the head withdrew and the curtains fell together again.

The curtains were still moving as one of the nurses pushed them open, but nothing was there—except the closed window, securely locked from the inside.

The screams of the second nurse brought the medical staff to the ward from all parts of the hospital, and again a thorough search was made without anything being discovered.

It was a closely locked ward. The outside windowsills were about nine feet from the ground, and beyond that was a

12-foot wall topped with iron spikes and a thick ledge of glass splinters. How could any intruder withdraw his head and shoulders and disappear within seconds, closing and locking the window from the opposite side?

Later the same day, after an emergency meeting, Phillips was removed to a private room. Two experienced nurses were assigned to him. Shortly after one in the morning, both nurses heard voices from within the private room, but every time they checked, Phillips was sound asleep and no one else was present.

Two hours later, they distinctly heard a loud chuckle, and to their horror saw a face protruding from between the curtains of the only window in the room. The description given by the nurses was the same as that of the person who had been seen before. As they stood rooted to the spot, the face laughed and then vanished.

The window, again, was securely locked. One of the nurses noticed that the temperature of the room had dropped considerably, although the radiators were so hot that it was impossible to touch them with bare hands.

Less than three hours later, John Phillips died. Never again did anyone in the hospital report hearing the strange murmuring voices, or the animal sounds, or seeing any mysterious visitors.

MESSAGES FROM BEYOND

Footsteps

A practical nurse, Phyllis Hudson has met a lot of odd people in very unusual circumstances. One of the strangest cases occurred in an old house in Westcott, near Darling, England.

The house stood in the center of what was once a rose garden, the pride of the neighborhood. The bushes, tended by the owner of the house, had been covered with luxuriant blooms. But since he died two years before, the garden had grown to weeds and it was too much for his widow to handle.

When the widow herself became seriously ill and was confined to bed, she required 24-hour care, so Mrs. Hudson was hired as a live-in nurse.

The widow's bedroom was on the second floor of the rambling two-story house. At first Mrs. Hudson slept in a small bedroom next to her charge. But she soon changed to a room at the opposite end of the house. The reason Mrs. Hudson changed rooms also kept relatives away from night visits to the widow. After seven p.m. no one came to see her, no matter how many might arrive during daylight hours.

The reason was the footsteps. At ten o'clock every night footsteps would be heard at the front door. Slowly, deliberately, they would cross the hall to the stairs and then start mounting them steadily.

At first, Mrs. Hudson thought it was an intruder. She stood at the head of the stairs and watched anxiously. But though she could hear the footsteps mounting higher and higher, she saw no one. She might have laid it all down to imagination, except for the family dog. When the footsteps started climbing upwards he would sit beside her at the top of the stairs, cowering, the thick ruff of hair on the back of his neck standing upright, a growl deep in his throat. He was obviously terrified.

As the footsteps came toward her, Mrs. Hudson could no longer stand her ground. She would back away from the stairs and hurry down the hall to her own room. With a final yap, the dog would follow her, tail between his legs.

The footsteps would reach the upper landing and go into the widow's bedroom. The only one not upset by the footsteps was the old woman herself, who said the invisible visitor was just her husband coming to make his nightly call.

One day the widow died, and from that moment the footsteps no longer sounded in the silent house. But to everyone's amazement, the dilapidated rose garden suddenly burst into huge fragrant blossoms more beautiful than anyone could remember having seen before.

People around there said it was the husband's way of giving his wife a royal welcome.

Monkeys in the Closet

Beatrice Straight, a prize-winning stage and film actress, lived in New York City, but often spent weekends at a house that had belonged to her late parents, in Old Westbury, Long Island.

It was a spooky old place, with many Oriental ornaments that had been collected by her father, Willard Straight.

He had been a U.S. consul in Manchuria, a region of China. He had also created a Chinese garden on the little estate.

Beatrice's thoughts were running to ghosts at this time, for she had recently appeared on Broadway in a scary play called, *The Innocents*. It was based on "Turn of the Screw," a famous ghost story by the writer Henry James. The story had been adapted for the stage by playwright William Archibald, who was also very interested in ghosts.

One weekend, Beatrice and her husband, Peter Cookson, brought a group of friends out from New York City, including William Archibald, to spend a country weekend. That evening, Archibald suggested that they do some table tipping. Beatrice recalls:

"Bill told us what to do, that the table would tip and tap out letters on the floor. For example, one tap equaled an A, five taps meant E, and so on through the alphabet. We went up to a bedroom my father had used and sat around a small table with our hands on top, and it suddenly started to go like mad, tipping and all.

"It said it was a spirit from the Gobi Desert. Sometimes the table would rise up above our heads, shaking, and then crash. We broke two tables that way. But before the second table broke, it spelled out:

MONKEYS IN THE CLOSET.

"I went to the closet in the room that I'd never looked in before. It was full of books that had been put there way back when. The table kept spelling out, MONKEYS IN THE CLOSET. I started pulling books out, and there at the back of the closet was an ivory statue with twelve monkeys on it. It was an ivory tree, and the monkeys were going up the tree."

By this time, everybody was getting pretty nervous. So when the table tapped out: BURY ME IN THE GARDEN, they thought that was a very good idea. They were eager to get the statue out of the house and out of sight. So the whole group took it out and buried it in the Chinese garden.

Half an hour later, Archibald went to his bedroom and came out to say somebody must be kidding him. For on his pillow he had found one of the little ivory monkeys. But then

everybody realized that the monkeys were not detachable. The statue was a solid block of ivory. The next morning, they found another ivory monkey on the steps of the front door.

When *The Innocents* had first been produced, famous psychic Eileen Garrett had been engaged as a consultant. Beatrice now went to her and told her what had happened.

"She said to go back and dig up the statue," Beatrice relates. "She said don't do these things unless you're with somebody who really knows what it is all about, that there are spirits who are naughty and can cause trouble."

The next weekend, Beatrice and her husband went to the Chinese garden to dig up the statue. And there was no statue there!

You Will Die at Midnight

Probably the most amazing case ever recorded of a death premonition concerned Thomas, Lord Lyttelton.

The remarkable events took place in November, 1779. Lyttelton had gone from London to his country house in Epsom, where he was convalescing after an illness. Walking in the large conservatory with Lady Affleck and her two daughters, Lyttelton noticed a robin perched on an orange tree close by. He tried to catch it, but failed. Seeing the ladies exchange amused glances, he vowed he would catch it—even if it killed him. After a long chase, he succeeded.

The next morning, Lyttelton appeared at the breakfast table, so pale and haggard that his guests anxiously asked him if anything was the matter. Finally, he told them a strange story.

The previous night, after he had lain awake for some time, he heard what sounded like the tapping of a bird at his window, followed by a gentle fluttering of wings in his room. Puzzled, he raised himself on an elbow and saw an amazing sight. In the center of the room stood a beautiful woman dressed in white, with a small robin perched like a falcon on her wrist. This woman told him to prepare for death as he had only a short time to live. When Lyttelton was able to speak, he asked how long he had. The phantom replied, "Not three days. And you will depart at the hour of twelve."

For two days Lyttelton fluctuated between despondency and hysterical gaiety. At dinner on Saturday, the third day, he amazed his guests with his wit and vitality. But afterward, he lapsed into a gloomy silence, and as the evening wore on, he grew restless. He could not sit still but paced restlessly to and fro, muttering incoherently. Every few minutes he took out his pocket watch, gazed at the time, and wiped beads of sweat from his forehead.

Eventually, when the hands of his watch read half-past

eleven, he went to his room, without a word of farewell to his guests. He had no idea that not only his own watch but every clock in the house had been put forward half an hour by well-meaning friends!

Sitting up in bed, watch in hand, Lyttelton awaited the fatal hour of midnight. As the minute hand slowly approached twelve, he asked to see his valet's watch and found that it showed the same time as his own.

With pounding heart and straining eyes he watched the minute hand draw nearer and nearer midnight. A minute to go—half a minute. Then it pointed to the fatal hour—and nothing happened. It crept slowly past. The crisis was over!

Lyttelton put down the watch with a sigh of relief, and then broke into wild, hysterical giggling. He spoke to his valet for ten minutes more and seemed to be his normal self once again, completely at ease.

Then he remembered his nightly dose of medicine and asked his valet to prepare it. As no spoon was at hand, the valet stirred it with the handle of a toothbrush that lay on the bedside table. Lyttelton scolded him for his dirty habits and ordered him to fetch a proper spoon.

When the servant returned a few minutes later, Lyttelton was lying back on his pillow, breathing heavily and with a strange, haunted look in his eyes. The valet ran downstairs to get help. The alarmed guests rushed to his room, but a few moments later, he was dead, the watch clutched in his hand pointing to half-past twelve. In reality, he had died on the very stroke of midnight.

Death in a Dark Mirror

Max Hellier was never able to explain exactly what it was that woke him from his normally deep sleep. He could usually sleep through any disturbance.

The room in the Munich inn where he was staying was pitch-black, and although there was no light of any sort from the window, a faint, bluish glimmer permeated the gloom. It was a weird pulsating reflection of light, unlike any Hellier had ever seen.

Then he noticed that the light was surrounding the reflection of the bedroom door in the mirror on the opposite wall. But it was something else that almost made his heart stop beating. Although he could see nobody beside him in the bed, a quick glance to the side showed a definite indentation of the pillow and the outline of a body beneath the blankets.

Even worse, there was a sudden intense coldness beside him—almost as if he were lying beside a corpse! He glanced in the mirror again and stifled a scream of horror. Hellier couldn't see his reflection in the dark mirror: instead there was another man—a burly, bearded, handsome man with a swarthy complexion. And at that instant, Hellier could hear the man's heavy breathing.

Then—still in the mirror—he saw the bedroom door open slowly and a woman peer in. Her eyes were fixed on the figure of the bearded man on the bed.

Hellier watched as she crept up to the man with a horrible, feline stealth and gripped the sleeper's throat with her long, bony fingers. He stared silently at the mirror as she squeezed the last breath of life from the hefty man. Then suddenly the hideous drama ended. The picture faded and Hellier was once more alone in the room.

Badly shaken by this experience, Hellier wished he had stayed somewhere else. He had disliked the room in the inn in Munich as soon as he saw it, especially the tall mirror that overshadowed the room, reflecting every movement, every tiny disturbance. Hellier, never slept on the left side of his bed, and now, as he sat shivering in the huge bed, staring at the empty mirror, he was grateful for his habit of sleeping on the right. He sank thankfully back onto the pillows and tried to blot the dreadful vision of murder from his mind.

In the morning, he was sure that he had either dreamed the incident or else that his tired brain had run riot. He would have left the inn that very day except that he met an old army buddy walking through Munich. Franz Braun was down on his luck. His heart had always been in painting, but Hellier knew he had little talent. Braun had no job, no money, and that very morning had been evicted from his lodgings.

Hellier offered Braun a meal at the inn and a night's lodging—not only out of friendship. Hellier wanted to see if Braun too would see the strange scene in the mirror!

It turned out that by 1952, Braun had changed little from his war days. He wined and dined lavishly on Hellier's money and spent the whole evening flirting with the barmaid. Hellier had already gone up to the room when Braun came bustling in.

"She had to get back to work," he told Hellier, "so we may as well turn in for the night."

Hellier nodded.

Braun said, "The girl warned me not to sleep on the left side of the bed. I wonder why."

Hellier had not told Braun about the apparitions in the mirror, but Braun was skeptical anyway about supernatural experiences. They settled down to sleep, Braun on the left side of the bed.

It was hours later when Hellier woke to find that the room was deadly cold and, in the mirror at the foot of the bed, the bedroom door glowed again with that ghostly light.

He stared at the reflection. There was no sign of himself or Braun in the mirror, but the form of the heavy, dark-skinned man was once more lying on the left-hand side. Hellier turned to look at the form beside him, but the face on the pillow was that of Franz Braun.

Hellier looked back to the mirror, and just as it had on the previous night, the door in the mirror opened slowly. The same gaunt, marble-like face peered in and, with brutish determination, the figure crept toward the bed, its face contorted with malice. The cruel white fingers settled once more on the throat beneath the man's bushy beard.

Hellier watched fascinated as the woman's hands clasped tighter and tighter. Then, as the shuddering form in the mirror grew still, both figures vanished.

Braun had not stirred at all during the drama, but now Hellier turned to his friend and shook him. Braun could not be roused. Alarmed, Hellier snapped on the light, and then he let out a cry of sheer terror.

Braun was dead. On his throat were two red marks, slowly fading from sight.

Hellier's scream roused everybody. The doctor who was called attributed Braun's death to heart failure, but Hellier knew that Braun had been as healthy as a young horse.

The next day he questioned the barmaid, who had warned Braun about sleeping on the left-hand side of the bed. The girl looked at him uncertainly before saying, “I was right to warn him, Herr Hellier. The last few people who slept on the left side of that bed died in exactly the same way . . .”

Ghost with the Bloodstained Hands

I’ll call them Jan and Mark Jackson, because they aren’t looking for publicity. In 1965 the couple was living in an apartment on the third floor of an old Colonial-style house on Decatur Street in the French Quarter of New Orleans. Jan and Mark loved their apartment, with its charming, old-fashioned air. They didn’t even mind most of the strange things that kept happening.

For instance, the clock on the living room mantel kept stopping every night at 3 a.m. and had to be reset every morning. And sometimes the Jacksons glimpsed a couple of shadowy figures that vanished as quickly as they appeared.

But there was one ghost that made them shiver. It was the ghost of a young woman in a filmy white gown that kept drifting

through the rooms, her pleading eyes wide with shock and horror, her bloodstained hands clasped against her breast. This ghost upset the Jacksons so much that they began to ask questions about the old house. The answers led them to a story about something that had happened in the apartment back in 1910. At that time a young married woman was renting the Jacksons' apartment, where she was secretly meeting her lover. One day both she and her lover disappeared. It was suspected that the woman's jealous husband had found out about the affair and murdered them. But since the bodies were never found, there could also be another simpler explanation—one that the husband suggested—that the two had simply run away together. So, after the first flurry of headlines, the newspapers had dropped the subject and the story was forgotten.

Because of the ghost with the bloodstained hands, the Jacksons were convinced it was a case of murder and that the bodies had been hidden somewhere nearby. But where? Mark got his answer the day he went up to the attic to get something he had stored away.

In a corner, he noticed several rotted floorboards. Planning to replace them, he pulled them out and found himself looking down at two skeletons in the space below. Lying side by side, they were grinning up at him with gaping jaws. On the rib cage of one lay the blood-encrusted knife that must have killed them.

The Jacksons talked it over and decided that since both murderer and murdered were long dead, there would be no purpose in announcing their find. That night, they secretly buried the skeletons in a single grave. From that time on, the ghost with the bloodstained hands walked no more. And the clock on the mantel—that had obviously been marking the hour of the murder—continued ticking the night through.

6

LOST SOULS

The Lady and the Time Warp

It was nine o'clock in the morning one day in 1963. The corridors in the White Building on the campus of Wesleyan University, in Lincoln, Nebraska, were filled with the clatter and chatter of students arriving for their first classes.

Colleen Buterbaugh, secretary to the university dean, had come over from the next building to deliver some papers to the office of a visiting professor from Scotland. She knew that the professor, James McNutt, wasn't in because she had phoned him, but thought she would put the papers on his desk.

When she opened the door to the small office, everything suddenly went quiet. She could no longer hear the noise of the students. In fact, the room itself looked different, somehow strange.

Glancing to the right, she saw a tall young woman with long hair. "It was puffed up," Colleen said, "like they used to wear before World War I. She was wearing a lacy blouse closed at the neck and long sleeves. A long black skirt hung to her ankles, and she was wearing old-time buckle shoes. She was going through a rack of music, apparently looking for something."

The room felt cold and clammy. Colleen looked out the window and felt like she was in a different time. Colleen was seeing things as they must have looked on the campus fifty years before. The tall trees were not tall. They were only a few yards high, as though they had been planted only a few years before. Across from the White Building stood the main library of the university, but it was not there now. There was no building there at all.

"The woman had her back to me," Colleen said. "She was reaching up into one of the shelves with her right hand and standing perfectly still. She wasn't at all aware of my presence. She never moved. She was not transparent, and yet I knew she wasn't real. While I was looking at her she just faded away—not parts of her body one at a time, but her whole body at once."

Shaken to the core, Colleen staggered back to the building next door. As her coworkers gathered around to hear her story, an elderly professor said:

"Why, that's a dead ringer for Clara Mills as she looked when she started teaching here." He said that Clara, a professor of music, had begun teaching at the university in 1911, and had died suddenly in her office in 1940.

Colleen was shown old faculty photographs, and she recognized the mysterious, ghostly woman in one of them. It was Clara Mills.

After Colleen's experience, somebody asked James McNutt, the visiting professor from Edinburgh, if he now had any fears about going into his office.

"None at all," said Professor McNutt. "I don't see why Scotland should have a corner on all the ghosts."

The Girl from Leigh Park

Outside Waterlooville, England, there's a stretch of road without sidewalks. It's quite dangerous for pedestrians and few are seen on it, especially after nightfall.

On a November evening in 1976, Robert Spensley and his wife were driving home. His wife was at the wheel, and as they reached a dangerous stretch of road, Spensley suddenly saw a girl in the fading light. She was standing directly in the path of the car and his wife was driving straight toward her. He yelled at her to stop or to swerve to miss the girl.

Mrs. Spensley gave her husband a peculiar look and went on driving. Her husband put his hands over his eyes and waited for the thud of impact. There was nothing. When he dared look again, the girl was gone. His wife was still driving calmly. She had seen nothing.

The next morning Spensley reported his strange experience to his co-workers. Several of them spoke up. They had also seen the girl on the road. They said that it was believed to be the ghost of a girl who had once lived in nearby Leigh Park. One evening, while trying to hitch a ride home, she had been struck down by a car and killed. Since that time, she had been seen by a number of motorists on the same stretch of road.

One of Spensley's friends had an even stranger story to tell about the girl from Leigh Park. He said he was driving home through a heavy rain when, as he passed the cemetery, he was flagged down by a young girl. She was wet, bedraggled, and very forlorn. She told him that she lived in Leigh Park and needed a lift. He opened the door for her and she climbed in. She gave him the address in Leigh Park, but after that little was said by either of them. In the pouring rain, he had to keep his eyes and all his attention on the road. Finally he was in Leigh Park at the address the girl had given him.

"Here we are," he said, bringing the car to a stop. He reached over to open the car door for the girl when, to his shock, he

saw that the seat was empty. The girl was gone, though the door was still shut and the window rolled up. For a second, he wondered if she had ever really been there.

Then he looked down at the seat where she had been sitting. It was sopping wet.

The Man Who Projected Himself

One of the weirdest and most baffling types of psychic phenomena is the inexplicable power of certain people to project themselves from one place to another. While they remain physically in one place, they may be seen many miles away—appearing, at least, to be quite real.

Perhaps the most extraordinary case was related at sea in 1860 by Captain John Clarke, master of the schooner Julia Hallock, trading between Cuba and New York. He had heard it from a seaman named Robert Bruce from Devon, England.

Bruce, according to Clarke, was an honest and upright man who would not have lied about anything. He was also a first-class seaman, having risen to first mate by the time he was 30.

Bruce had been serving on a vessel plying from Liverpool,

England, to New Brunswick, in eastern Canada. His strange experiences took place after six weeks at sea. Darkness had fallen and Bruce went to the captain's cabin to work out some navigational calculations.

Bruce, intent upon his figures, did not notice that the captain stepped out of the cabin. When he had figured out his equation, he announced their present longitude and latitude without looking up. Receiving no reply, he raised his head and was astonished to see that not only had the captain left, but that a complete stranger was sitting at the writing table.

Bruce was a man of more than average courage, but the sight of the strange man's keen eyes boring into his filled him with sudden apprehension. He did not stop to ask questions but fled and sought out the captain, who was back on the bridge.

Seeing Bruce's white face, the captain commented, "You look as if you've seen a ghost."

Bruce said: "Who is that man sitting at your desk, sir—in your cabin?"

The captain stared. "There is no man in my cabin—and if you saw anyone you must be seeing things, Mr. Bruce."

When Bruce insisted that he had seen a strange man, the captain suggested that it must have been another crew member.

"It was not, sir—I know every man in the crew well enough to know that this man was a complete stranger to me," Bruce insisted.

The captain, realizing his mate was in earnest, ordered Bruce to go back to his cabin and ask the stranger to step up to the bridge. But Bruce was afraid now, without knowing precisely why. He said he would rather not go back to the cabin alone.

At first the captain was angry and ordered Bruce not to be ridiculous. Finally he went down to the cabin with Bruce. It was empty. But then they both saw some writing on the captain's slate. The words were: Steer to the Nor'West.

The captain called to the cabin every man who might have entered it while he was away, and made each in turn write out the same words. None matched the writing on the slate.

"Do you believe in ghosts, Mr. Bruce?" the captain asked.

Bruce said he did not.

"Nor do I believe in such things," said the captain. "But all the same, I think we will sail that way—just to see what does happen."

In the middle of the next afternoon, the lookout reported sighting an iceberg. When the captain and Bruce trained their glasses on it, they saw a vessel trapped in the ice.

The ship was a schooner on her way from Quebec to Liverpool with about 60 passengers. Water and food were dangerously low. The crew and passengers were in a sorry plight. Had Bruce's ship not sailed in their direction, all might have died of starvation and exposure.

Bruce was on deck supervising the rescue operation when one man in a very weak condition was hoisted aboard. Bruce went to assist him, and when the passenger lifted his head, Bruce recognized the face. It was the very same man he had seen sitting in the captain's cabin—miles from that spot!

When he was feeling stronger, the passenger was asked to go to the cabin and write on the slate the words Steer to the Nor'West. He did so, and the writing was found to be exactly the same!

The passenger obviously could not have written the message, trapped as he was on the ice-bound ship. And when asked, he said that he did not recall even having a dream in which he wrote such a message.

But the captain of the wrecked vessel reported that at the hour when Bruce saw the stranger in the cabin, the man had been in a very deep sleep. When he awoke, he had said something strange: "Captain, we shall be rescued very soon now—by sunset tomorrow at the very latest."

And the passenger went on to tell the captain that he had dreamed of being aboard a strange ship that was coming to the rescue. He even described the ship in detail as he came out of his deep, trance-like sleep—although he did not remember the dream ten minutes later. The description, which the captain remembered distinctly, fitted Bruce's ship exactly.

The Stuffed Dog

Priory House stands on the Isle of Wight, part of the British Isles. A lovely old house, it is called "Priory" because it was built on the foundations of what was once a Chinese monastery. Something of the peaceful atmosphere of the monastery seems to pervade the old house. Something also haunts it—the ghost of a young girl.

Her portrait hangs in the dining room. It shows a 14- or 15-year-old sitting on a garden seat. She is dressed in a long, blue gown in the style of the early 1700s. A satin ribbon fastens a little canary to her wrist. At her feet lies a small furry dog, a King Charles spaniel. The young girl must have lived in the house at one time, but so long ago that nobody remembers who she was.

Both the girl and her canary have gone to their graves. But the dog remains. Stuffed, he sits in a glass case that is set over the main staircase. From there he surveys the rooms of Priory House with a penetrating stare whenever the light hits his glass eyes.

As for the Little Lady in Blue, as she came to be called, the grave couldn't hold her. She has been seen several times, a faint shadowy figure either on the staircase or in the gardens. She comes with a whiff of lavender perfume, bringing a breath of happiness, a light suggestion of tinkling laughter, the soft swish of silken skirts, and the faint patter of light footsteps as she skips at play.

For many years, the house was occupied by old Miss Laura, who cherished it. Most especially she felt a deep affection for the gentle, happy ghost. Then Miss Laura died. Since she left no heirs, the house was sold by the estate to a wealthy American woman. The new owner poured money into renovations. Most of the old furniture was sold. In its place antiques from different historical periods were bought and the rooms redecorated. The portrait of the Little Lady in Blue stayed, but the dog in its glass case went.

When the Americans moved in with a large staff of servants, the tranquil atmosphere of the old house was gone. Now the servants were wakened at night by the sound of a child's feet clattering down the corridors, a child's voice crying between heartrending sobs, "Where is my dog? My little dog, where is he? I want my dog!"

The servants were distracted. One by one they left. Last to go was the butler, who had worked for the American woman for many years. He told his employer unhappily that he could no longer bear the noises that were setting his nerves on edge.

Something had to be done, but what? Perhaps friends of old Miss Laura would know the answer. The American invited two of them for tea one day and plied them with questions. Why was a child racketing through the halls crying for her dog? What dog?

That was when they told her about the little stuffed dog in the glass case, the stuffed dog that was disposed of when the house was sold. Where was it now?

The American woman was nothing if not determined. She sent out tracers for the little dog, leaving no clue unchecked. Finally she found it in an antique shop in a town many miles away. She bought it and returned it to its place above the stairwell. With its return, the noises stopped. Once more there was only the occasional patter of happy feet, a child's light tinkle of laughter, the soft swish of silk passing down the halls, contented sounds that troubled no one.

The American woman has long since sold the Priory. It was bought by a travel organization that had no trouble booking guests who were attracted by the Priory's quaint loveliness, its tranquil atmosphere and, most especially, by the stories of the happy little ghost. Hundreds passed through the old house.

Now and then management changed. But each manager who arrived to take over the job was given a stern warning:

"If you want to keep the peace, never, never remove the stuffed dog in the glass case from its spot over the stairwell."

Where Is My Daughter?

One of the saddest ghosts I've heard of was that of an elderly woman. Back in the 1800s she and her husband had moved from Ireland to Australia, where they settled on the west coast near the town of Fremantle. Widowed early, the woman had a beautiful young daughter with red hair and a sweet Irish face. One day her daughter was abducted.

The mother searched for the lost girl frantically until, wild with grief, she went insane and was locked up in the gloomy buildings that made up the asylum at Fremantle. There she spent her days wandering the halls of her prison hospital, still searching. Then one day she ended her life by throwing herself out of a first-story window that was more than ten feet above the rocky ground. But her spirit still could not rest. Even after the asylum buildings were renovated to house a museum and an adjacent art center, the old woman continued to haunt their halls, searching for her lost daughter.

A number of people have come face to face with her—a frail

wraith that vanished before their eyes. She always wore the same thing—a plain black dress with a white collar and lace frills down the front. A delicate Victorian-style cap framed her face.

Museum employees working late at night reported seeing her. Her image was lit by the ghostly lantern she carried, gliding noiselessly through the darkened corridors. Teachers grading papers late at night at the local high school would look down to see a flickering light moving from window to window of the old buildings. And they would whisper to one another that the poor woman was walking again.

Then, on March 19, 1980, Shelley, a young college student, came to the asylum to fulfill an assignment for her photography class. She was to shoot the various rooms of the art center. In one room, trying for an interesting shot, she turned her camera toward the windows. Through the lens she saw, peering back at her, the demented face of an elderly woman in a lace cap. The window in which the face appeared was more than ten feet above ground level—too high for anyone to play such an elaborate hoax.

Shelley thought at first it might have been just her imagination. But when she had the film developed, there was the face, just as she had seen it through her camera lens.

Shelley's photo was published in the local newspaper and created quite a stir. Photographers of all kinds flocked to the art center in hopes of capturing the old woman's image on film again. None were successful.

In the years that followed, the old woman's wispy figure was no longer seen in the halls of the old asylum. At night the windows were no longer illuminated by the flickering light of her lantern. Why?

Could it be that, looking through the window into the face of the girl behind the camera, she thought she had found her long-lost daughter at last? For Shelley is an Irish girl with beautiful red hair and dancing Irish eyes.

7 DANGEROUS DEMONS

A Very Scary Doll

Can a doll haunt a house?

Take Robert, a large doll that for many years inhabited the Artist House in Key West, an island off the southern tip of Florida. The Artist House is a bed and breakfast establishment, a place to relax, but some patrons have had anything but relaxing times there.

The owner, Ed Cox, tells of a young German woman who stayed in the front bedroom, and who was terrified. "The more you go up that staircase, the worse the feeling is," she said.

The front bedroom was the place where the doll had been kept for many years.

A plumber working at the Artist House insisted that he heard the doll giggle, and that he found it sitting in different spots when no one was around to move it. Did it move itself?

Owner Cox tells of other disturbances in the house, including pictures that fly off the walls. He once saw the door of a book cabinet spring open for no visible reason. Sometimes doors won't open. Sometimes they open when they shouldn't.

Who is Robert, and what could he be up to?

Robert was the doll of Robert Gene Otto, an artist who lived in the house all his life. When Gene, as he was called, was given the doll he was five years old. It was the custom around 1900 to give a child a doll that looked like him.

Robert the doll is the size of a child. He has human hair, and buttons for eyes. Gene used to dress the doll in his own clothes. He also gave it his first name.

Myrt Reuter, who owned the house after Gene died, cared for Robert as though he were a human being. "It has different kinds of clothes," she said. "It was in a pixie outfit when I got him. Now I have Gene's little sailor suit on him."

"I've been told," she said, "that when Gene did anything mean or hateful he always blamed it on the doll."

Myrt Reuter tells of renting the house to a law student

one winter. She says, “He told this story that the doll was voodoo and it locked him up in the attic.”

Was that true? Possibly. But it is a fact that many people have reported strange experiences in the house, whether or not Robert was causing them.

Enid Hoffman, who has written books about the Hawaiian mystical tradition, Huna, suspects that what is going on with Robert is what the Hawaiians call Mana.

“Mana,” she says, “carries ideas. It can be stored in certain things, wood and silk in particular. It flows in ways that are hard for us to understand. The doll has possibly infected the atmosphere of the house.”

Gene had been a bad-tempered person all his life. The doll had been his “mirror image.” A lot of his personality had gone into the doll—all the evil thoughts and actions. Possibly Gene’s anger is living on after his death, through Robert.

The Portrait

A few years after World War I, a prominent Boston artist was a house guest in the home of a Mr. Izzard. He was given the best room in the old family mansion that stood on the outskirts of Boston. It was a large bedroom on the top floor with side windows that looked out on landscaped gardens.

The first night he was awakened suddenly by a brilliant glow: it hurt his eyes and made his flesh crawl. In that light he saw a woman in an elegant gown standing at the side of the room. Fascinated, he watched as she hurled something out of the window. He couldn't see what it was.

Then the woman turned around and looked at him. She would have been beautiful if her face had not been set in such hard, cruel lines. Dark, malignant eyes flashed their hatred. Her lips were pursed in a smirk of triumph. As the gloating face stared at him, the light and figure slowly faded and disappeared.

The next two nights the horrible vision repeated itself. After the third appearance, the artist felt compelled to sketch the face of the woman he had seen. Later he showed the drawing to his city friends. Everyone was disturbed by the evil in it.

Several months later, Mr. Izzard again invited the artist to his home. This time he led his friend through a gallery of portraits of his ancestors. The artist stopped suddenly before one of the paintings. It was the portrait of a beautiful and demure young woman.

"I've met her somewhere I'm sure," he exclaimed. "I'd know that face anywhere—only—"

Mr. Izzard laughed. "You couldn't have known her," he said. "She's been dead for a hundred years. She was my great-grandfather's second wife and she certainly was no credit to the family."

He went on to explain that his great-grandfather's first wife had died, leaving behind her little son. His second wife, having given birth to her own son, was filled with jealousy; sure the

family property would go to the older boy. One day the older boy's crumpled body was found below the window of the bedroom where the artist had seen the vision. The child had died instantly of a broken neck.

"She was suspected of having murdered him," Mr. Izzard explained. "But nothing could ever be proved."

"It can now," the artist exclaimed. Describing what he had seen, he went to get the drawing he had made.

To his horror, Mr. Izzard saw that the features of the woman in the sketch were the exact features of the woman in the portrait.

The Power at Nagoon Park

In the daytime Nagoon Park seems a pleasant enough place, lying almost four miles away from the town of Manistee on the western side of Lake Michigan. It's woodsy with meadowlands, the home of birds and squirrels, bright and busy. But at dusk a different atmosphere settles over the silent acres. Then it becomes haunted, dark and foreboding. There are accounts of lights flickering, and jumbles of voices and screams of a woman and children, carried on sudden gusts of wind that seem to rise from nowhere.

Brian Williams, a newcomer to town, had heard all kinds of

stories about the park. Some said it was once the sacred haunt of ancient Indian shamans, who practiced their secret rituals in it. Others spoke of a witches' cult performing strange ceremonies there after dark. And then there was the horrible account of a farmer who once lived there with his wife and a brood of children. One night, in a mad rage, the farmer murdered the whole family, swinging right and left with a bloody axe.

Whatever the reason, all could agree on the dark nature of the park. So bad was its reputation that the city ordered it closed at dusk: the only park in the whole area that was shut down after sunset.

When Brian first heard all these stories, he was amused by them. Well educated and with a college degree, he was not given to what he considered superstition. One day he decided to put an end to all the town lore with a little commonsense action. He'd drive out to Nagoon Park at dusk and prove there was nothing in the tales. Though the park was closed, he'd get as close to it as possible and spend the night.

It wasn't hard to find other recruits, but he was able to convince his girlfriend and another skeptical young couple. They decided to make a lark of it. At dusk they piled into Brian's car and drove down the country road in high spirits, stopping as close to the park entrance as they could.

Outside the car all was silent and motionless. The dark shapes of trees in the park hovered high against the sky like a wall, vague, menacing. The air had an uncanny stillness. The heavy silence seemed to flow out of the park like a thick tide. The voices of the young people sounded loud in the night. There was a shrill, almost hysterical cackle to their laughter.

Then, in the stillness, something outrageous happened. The rear of the car started to rise. The couples fell silent, staring at one another. Was it their imagination? Surely it couldn't really be happening.

Higher and higher rose the back of the car. Brian found himself sliding against the steering wheel, staring down at the hood, which was slanting noticeably downwards. And still the rear of the car kept rising until it was some four or five feet above the ground and almost perpendicular to the road. It would have

taken a crane to lift the car, yet the country road was silent and deserted.

Then, all at once, the car was dropped. It fell with a crash. The girl on the back seat was flung against the top of the car. She had been too shocked to utter a sound before, but now she began howling with pain and terror. Brian was shaking as he turned the key in the ignition. The car started! He raced it down the dirt road back to Manistee.

Brian has never returned to Nagoon Park. And he no longer laughs at the tales told about it. He has his own story now.

Killer Sound Waves from the Sky

One gray February day in 1965, a flock of pigeons winged over the woods near Warminster in England's rural Wiltshire. Suddenly, the winter calm was splintered by a vibrant high-pitched hum that came, as witnesses later testified, "out of the sky."

As though struck by some giant fist, the birds faltered in

mid-air, struggled to regain formation, and then fell, like a shower of stones into the trees below. Every pigeon was dead, apparently killed instantaneously by mysterious waves of sound.

There was a government investigation, but no scientific theorizing could explain the attacks on both animals and humans from something violent and invisible in the sky. The file is still open.

But this was not the first time an event like this had happened. It began in the early hours of Christmas Day, 1964, when people were jerked abruptly from their sleep by strange, frightening noises above the rooftops.

A witness said later: "There were crashes, thuds and clatters, as though someone was bombarding the houses with gigantic rocks—and in the background was a high-pitched hum, vibrating on the frosty air."

But outside in the darkness, nothing could be seen, although stone walls shook with echoing vibrations.

Then suddenly, the noises stopped. Puzzled and alarmed, the people of Warminster went back to bed. Some blamed the army: there was a military camp near Warminster. But the army didn't usually carry out exercises on Christmas Day, and the mysterious sounds did not remotely resemble explosions.

The sonic bombardments lasted for six hours on that memorable morning. No one could come up with a reasonable explanation. But the noises seemed to have died away—for good, it was hoped.

Then, in February, 1965, the sounds from the sky began again, with the strange mid-air massacre of pigeons. And this time the attacks began to take a vicious turn.

One person who felt their full fury was a 19-year-old farmer who was walking along a dark, deserted road after seeing his girlfriend home. The night was silent, all sound blanketed by dense fog.

At first, the youth didn't take much notice of a faint humming noise. Then it swelled into a shrill, ear-splitting screech, "as though all the devils in hell had been let loose."

All at once, a fearsome, bone-crushing pressure clamped down on the young man, forcing him to his knees in the road.

An icy, stinging wind tore at his face, and noiseless waves of inexplicable pressure buffeted his body. His head felt as though it were held in iron clamps. Then the pressure lifted, as suddenly as it had descended, and he staggered home. His parents took one look at his white, terrified face and sent for the doctor, who treated the young man for severe shock.

Animals suffered most severely from the assaults. After one weird burst of ultrasound, dozens of field mice were found lying dead in a field. Their fur was singed and their bodies perforated with tiny holes. Dogs and cats became ill, and canaries and budgerigars toppled dead from their perches.

The violent sound attacks lasted—on and off—until the end of June, 1965. Scientists and government investigators arrived at Warminster and the surrounding area to study the phenomenon and came away baffled.

Is there any rational explanation? Were the sound waves that battered Warminster a product of natural causes—or something else? And can it be pure coincidence that the place in Britain where the greatest numbers of corroborated UFO sightings have occurred is Warminster?

8

CURSES

The Curse of the Witches of Skye

A cold, wintry gale was howling outside, as Margaret Fraser lay on the couch in front of the peat fire in the cottage where she and her husband, Norman, lived on the west coast of Scotland's Isle of Skye. It was December, 1900.

Margaret was expecting her fourth child, and since her husband, a shepherd, was out on the hillside, Mrs. Mackinnon, a neighbor, had come in to help tend the youngest of the Frasers' three children, Morag, a little girl about a year old.

Both women were drowsy. Soon Mrs. Mackinnon nodded off, lulled by the warmth of the glowing peat fire.

Margaret Fraser was almost asleep too, when she heard a low muttering. She opened her eyes and saw three ugly little old women sitting around the fire, whispering together, as they admired the sleeping child. They were certainly not women from the neighborhood. Then Margaret suddenly understood: these were no ordinary visitors. They were witches who had come to harm the baby.

Margaret pretended to sleep while one of the hags got up, reached out for the child, and said to the others: "We will take her away and leave at once."

The other two disagreed. "You have so many from this house already," countered one. "Better instead to put a curse on her."

So the first witch cast a spell.

"When this sod of peat shall burn away, that child shall die and go to clay." And she hurled a piece of peat into the fire.

Then the witches vanished. Margaret rose quickly from her couch, took the piece of peat from the fire and extinguished it in a pail of water. Then, wrapping the peat in a rag, she locked it away in a chest and hoped that she had beaten the awful curse.

The chest and its dreadful secret remained a mystery in the family for more than 20 years. Morag, the baby girl, grew up to be a beautiful young woman who eventually became engaged to a handsome young man.

It was the custom in the islands in those days that an engaged girl did not attend church from the day of her betrothal until the day of her marriage.

So one Sunday, while her parents attended church, Morag felt more tempted than ever to have a look in the old chest that her mother always kept locked and hidden in the cupboard.

She found a screwdriver and forced it open. She saw nothing unusual inside, except a piece of charred peat, wrapped in a rag.

She couldn't imagine what possessed her mother to keep a piece of peat so carefully concealed in a chest. She had never heard it spoken of in the family.

Morag could not think of any better use for the piece of peat than to toss it on the fire.

No sooner had the peat begun to burn than the girl grew afraid. She was seized with a strange feeling that something was going to happen to her.

Meanwhile, Morag's parents were making their way home from church. As they walked they heard an oystercatcher down by the shore crying, "Kleep-kleep." This bird, when in flight, looks like a black-and-white cross. Its melancholy cry was taken as a warning of imminent disaster.

Getting nearer home, the Frasers heard their dog whining anxiously and saw the animal running around the house, obviously excited. They ran to the cottage.

Inside they found Morag. She was dying from no visible cause. There was no sign of the peat that the witches had cursed more than 20 years before. It had burned to nothing. The fate that Morag had been saved from in her infancy had caught up with her at last.

The Mummy's Curse

The Princess of Amen-Ra lived some 1,500 years before our modern calendar began. When she died, she was placed in an ornate wooden coffin and buried deep in a vault at Luxor, on the banks of the Nile.

Had she been left undisturbed in her vault, perhaps this would have been the end of the story. In fact, it was only the beginning. For ten years before the start of the 20th century, the evil influence of her coffin brought death and havoc wherever it went.

Of all tales of the supernatural this one is perhaps the best documented, the most disturbing, and the most difficult to explain.

In the late 1890s, four rich young Englishmen visiting the excavations at Luxor were invited to buy an exquisitely fashioned mummy case containing the remains of the Princess of Amen-Ra.

They drew lots. The winner paid several hundred pounds and had the coffin taken to his hotel. A few hours later he was seen walking out toward the desert. He was never seen again.

The next day, one of his companions was shot by an Egyptian servant. The wound was so severe that his arm had to be amputated. The third man in the party found on his return home that the bank holding his entire savings had failed. The fourth man suffered a severe illness, lost his job, and was reduced to selling matches in the street.

Eventually, the coffin reached England, where it was bought by a London businessman. After three members of his family had been injured in a road accident, and his house severely

damaged by fire, the owner of the coffin donated it to the British Museum.

Despite its reputation, the authorities agreed to accept the gift. But the Princess of Amen-Ra was not long in bringing calamity to her new home. As the coffin was being unloaded from a truck in the museum courtyard, the truck suddenly went into reverse, trapping a passerby, who was taken to a hospital.

Then, as the casket was being lifted up the stairs by two workmen, one fell and broke his leg. The other man, in his thirties and apparently in perfect health, died unaccountably two days later.

Somehow, the Princess was installed in the Egyptian Room. Night watchmen at the museum frequently heard frantic hammering and sobbing coming from the coffin. Other exhibits in the room were hurled about. On one occasion a keeper claimed that he had been attacked by a spirit who leaped out of the casket and tried to hurl him down a delivery chute with a forty-foot drop.

Cleaning personnel at the museum refused to go near the Princess of Amen-Ra after one man derisively flicked a dust cloth at the face painted on the coffin and his child died of measles soon afterward.

Finally, the museum authorities had the mummy moved to the basement, where it could surely do no further harm. Within a week, one of the moving men was seriously ill, and the supervisor of the move was found dead at his desk.

By now the papers had seized the story. A staff photographer took a picture of the mummy case and found when he developed it that the painting on the coffin had changed into a human—and horrifying—face. The photographer went home, locked his door, and shot himself.

The museum then sold the mummy to a private collector. After continual misfortune, he banished it to the attic, where it was languishing when Madame Helena Blavatsky, a well-known authority on the occult, visited the house. She did not know the history of the mummy, or that it was even on the premises. Yet as soon as she entered the house, she was seized with a fit of shivering and declared there was an evil influence of incredible intensity at work.

The host, almost jokingly, invited her to have a look around. Madame Blavatsky searched the house without success, until she came to the attic and found the mummy case. She knew at once that this was the source of the evil influence she had felt.

"Would you be able to exorcise this evil spirit?" asked the host.

"There is no such thing as exorcism in this case," replied Madame Blavatsky. "Evil remains evil forever. Nothing can be done about it. I implore you to rid yourself of this evil thing as soon as possible."

The owner of the house did not take the matter seriously until a week or so later, when a member of his family, moving some suitcases in the attic, claimed to have seen a figure rise from the mummy case and glide across the floor. After this, he decided to take Madame Blavatsky's advice and get rid of the disturbing object.

No British museum would take the mummy; the fact that nearly 20 people had met with death or disaster from handling the casket was now well known.

Eventually, an unsuperstitious, hard-headed American archaeologist who dismissed the happenings as quirks of circumstance paid a very handsome price for the specimen. He then made arrangements for its removal to New York. In April 1912, the collector escorted his prize aboard a sparkling new White Star liner about to make its maiden voyage to New York.

On the night of April 14, amid scenes of unprecedented horror, the Princess Amen-Ra accompanied 1,500 passengers to their deaths at the bottom of the Atlantic. The name of the ship was the Titanic.

Revenge of the Waterford Ghost

It's not often that a ghost has a chance to get revenge on people who are still alive, but near Waterford, New York, one supposedly did just that.

Around the year 1900, a carpenter lived near the end of a barge canal. He was poor and sick with tuberculosis, but he still worked hard to support his wife and two children with earnings from odd jobs about the village.

Unfortunately, his own parents were particularly selfish, cruel, and mercenary. They demanded that he will them his house and property, which in case of his death should have gone to his wife. This, of course, the carpenter refused to do. Shortly before he died, however, he warned his parents that if they did anything to harm his family after he was gone, he would come back and haunt them as long as they lived. He would see to it, he said, that they would never make any profit from his house even if they did get it away from his wife.

As soon as their son had passed away, the parents undertook legal proceedings and managed to obtain possession of the property, evicting the impoverished wife and youngsters. The house was run-down, but usable, and they hoped to rent it rather quickly. So they closed the blinds and waited for a tenant. But no tenant ever rented it, for strange things began to happen.

Some of the neighbors, passing the empty house late at night, noticed lights shining between the shuttered windows and from between loose boards along the sides. At first they thought that perhaps the wife had come back and was living there secretly. They had liked the wife, so they did not investigate too carefully.

However, the lights started to wave about and flicker from within, far too mysteriously for comfort, and people began to cross the road when they passed that way after dark. Rumor spread that the son was making good his promise to keep his parents from making any money from the cottage. As no one wanted to rent the place, it fell more and more into disrepair. Even in its last years, when it was completely uninhabitable, the mysterious lights could still be seen.

The greedy parents nevertheless kept trying to rent or sell the place. No one would listen to them. The lights continued showing right up until the day when, with a muffled crash and a cloud of dry dust, the sagging roof fell in and the tottering walls collapsed into the cellar hole. Only then did the lights vanish, never to return.

No one could explain the mysterious lights, but many neighbors felt sure that the Waterford Ghost had gotten its revenge.

9

BANSHEE BODIES

The Disembodied Arm

Major MacGregor was a brave man. He had faced shot and shell and enemy soldiers in battle. But now he was terrified. This was something very different!

It was a night in 1871, and he was lying in bed in the elegant house of a cousin in Dublin, Ireland. He had been visiting his cousin when her husband became ill, and MacGregor had sat up with him several nights. But now the man seemed better, and MacGregor went to bed, asking a servant to call him if his host took a turn for the worse.

MacGregor, exhausted, fell asleep immediately. An hour later, he felt a push on his shoulder. He started up, thinking it was the servant.

"Is anything wrong?" he asked in the darkened room.

He got no answer, only another push.

The major got exceedingly annoyed. "Speak, man," he bellowed, "and tell me if anything is wrong!"

He still got no reply, but he had a feeling he was going to get another push. He twisted around in bed, reached out and grasped what seemed to be a human hand. It was warm and soft, a woman's hand.

"Who are you?" he demanded, but got no answer.

He tried to pull the hand toward him, but the owner of the hand seemed quite strong.

Thoroughly irritated, MacGregor exclaimed, "I am determined to find out who you are!"

He held the hand tightly in his right hand and with his left began to feel the wrist and arm. They seemed to be clothed in a tight-fitting sleeve, with a linen cuff.

When he got to the elbow, there was nothing more! All trace of the rest of the arm had disappeared! MacGregor was so astonished that he let go of the hand.

The next morning, he told of his strange experience. His hostess took his tale calmly.

His cousin said, "Oh that was old Aunt Betty. She lived in the upper part of the house and died many years ago."

Aunt Betty had been a very nice person, she assured him, and so there was nothing to worry about.

But when MacGregor talked with the servants, they were not so encouraging. Sometimes, they said, Aunt Betty's arm pulled the bedclothes off. One lady had received a slap in the face from an invisible hand.

MacGregor's cousin insisted that Aunt Betty would never think of hurting anyone. Maybe so, MacGregor reflected silently, but she just might scare you to death.

Evil Hands

During the time that Amanda was a member of the staff on Quarantine Station, she often said she wasn't afraid of the ghosts that people claimed to have seen there. She wasn't afraid, that is, until the night one tried to kill her.

Back in Colonial times, the Station was established on the rocky North Point of Manly Peninsula, a suburb of Sydney, Australia. When epidemics broke out on ships bringing

immigrants to Australia, everyone aboard was quarantined at Manly Cove until the danger of contagion was past. Few survived the quarantine period.

Today Quarantine Station is a national park. The old whitewashed buildings used as hospital and isolation wards have been preserved as landmarks. But something else seems to have survived, too—the ghosts of those who died here. So many sightings have been reported that guides regularly conduct ghost tours through the sprawling grounds.

Whether anyone sees a ghost or not, almost everyone admits to feeling the eerie atmosphere that settles upon Quarantine Station after dark. The spell is so strong that even members of the staff make sure to leave with the last tour group every night.

Only Amanda chose to remain. She couldn't imagine why anyone should fear the spirits of the gentle, suffering settlers who were buried here, and she loved the lonely beauty of the grounds. She was so confident of her safety that she made one of the isolation wards her living quarters, spending nights as well as days in it.

Then, one horrifying night of bright moonlight, everything changed. Amanda went for a walk along the coastal cliffs that fall away from the headlands on which Quarantine Station stands. She lingered there, reveling in the silence, gazing across the dark harbor at the lights of Sydney, as the moonlight spread its mysterious web over the dreaming land and sea.

All at once her mood was shattered. A presence hot and evil seemed to be pressing close against her. Strong hands suddenly struck her in the middle of her back. They began shoving her forward with tremendous force.

Amanda's feet scrabbled on the rocky cliff edge as she fought to regain her balance. Far below she could see the white line of surf breaking silver against the rocks. She knew that if she went down she would be bashed to death on those rocks. She had to get free. But no matter how hard she struggled, she couldn't break away from the thing that was pushing her so relentlessly forward.

Now her feet were beginning to slide over the brink. Pebbles were being dislodged. She could hear the clattering of the stones on the rocks below and knew she was about to follow them. She was down to her last chance.

Gathering up all the strength she had, Amanda flung herself backwards. The cruel hands loosened, their force spent. Amanda whirled around to see who was there. There was nothing! Everything was quiet and hushed as before.

Terrified, Amanda fled back along the footpath that had seemed so friendly only minutes before. She stumbled and fell and got up again and ran, gasping, all the way until she reached the safety—would it ever be safe again?—of the isolation ward.

Early the next day she resigned from her job and left Quarantine Station forever. Those invisible, cruel hands had reminded her of something she had forgotten. The first shipload of passengers to be detained at Quarantine Station had been convicts—and some among them had been violent criminals.

INDEX